WHO
IS THE
WORLD
FOR?

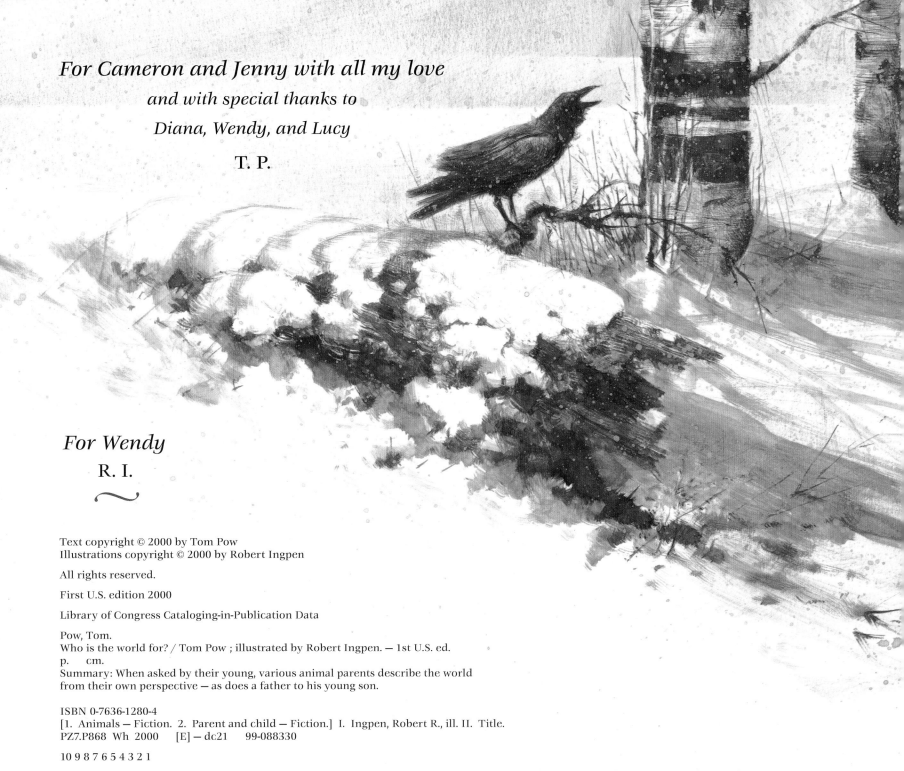

For Cameron and Jenny with all my love
and with special thanks to
Diana, Wendy, and Lucy
T. P.

For Wendy
R. I.

Text copyright © 2000 by Tom Pow
Illustrations copyright © 2000 by Robert Ingpen

First U.S. edition 2000

Library of Congress Cataloging-in-Publication Data

Pow, Tom.
Who is the world for? / Tom Pow ; illustrated by Robert Ingpen. — 1st U.S. ed.
p.   cm.
Summary: When asked by their young, various animal parents describe the world
from their own perspective — as does a father to his young son.

ISBN 0-7636-1280-4
[1. Animals — Fiction. 2. Parent and child — Fiction.] I. Ingpen, Robert R., ill. II. Title.
PZ7.P868 Wh 2000   [E] — dc21   99-088330

10 9 8 7 6 5 4 3 2 1

Printed in Belgium

This book was typeset in Veljovic. The illustrations were done in watercolor and pencil.

Candlewick Press, 2067 Massachusetts Avenue, Cambridge, Massachusetts 02140

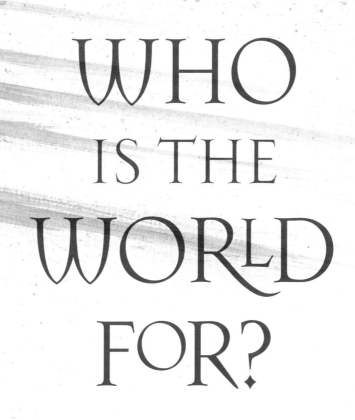

WHO
IS THE
WORLD
FOR?

TOM POW

illustrated by ROBERT INGPEN

CANDLEWICK PRESS
CAMBRIDGE, MASSACHUSETTS

Who is the world for?

the baby bear asks her mother
as she snuggles into her furry tummy
at the mouth of their winter cave.

Why, look around you,
the mother replies. The world
with all its deep dark caves
for you to shelter in, with all its
spring rivers, shining in sunlight,
shimmering with fish, and with all
its forests you'll never be lost in,
no matter how very far they stretch~

the world is for you!

Who is the world for?

the lion cub asks his father
as they lie together in the sun
and the father sniffs the dry, hot air.

Why, look around you, the father replies.

The world with all its grassy plains for you to run on,

with all its zebra and antelope and elephant for you to grow strong among

and with all its high smooth rocks for you to bask on~

how can you doubt that

the world is for you!

Who is the world for?

the baby hippo asks his mother
as they lie together, so close in the water
their backs are like stepping stones.

Why, look around you, gurgles his mother.

    The world with all its wide, slow brown rivers for you to dance in

and with all its deep muddy pools for you to wallow in, so cool

    in the midday sun even the elegant

antelope come down to drink~

    the world is for you!

Who is the world for?

    the baby whale asks her mother
as they swim side by side
    like a tugboat in the shadow
of an ocean liner.

Why, look around you,
sings her mother. The world
with all its deep roomy seas for you
to voyage through, all its million-kinded fish
that will part for you, all its rich seaweed,
its watery lights, its sea sounds
that speak so clearly to you~

the world is for you!

Who is the world for?

the baby Arctic hare asks her father
as they cozy together from the wind
in a warm burrow of snow.

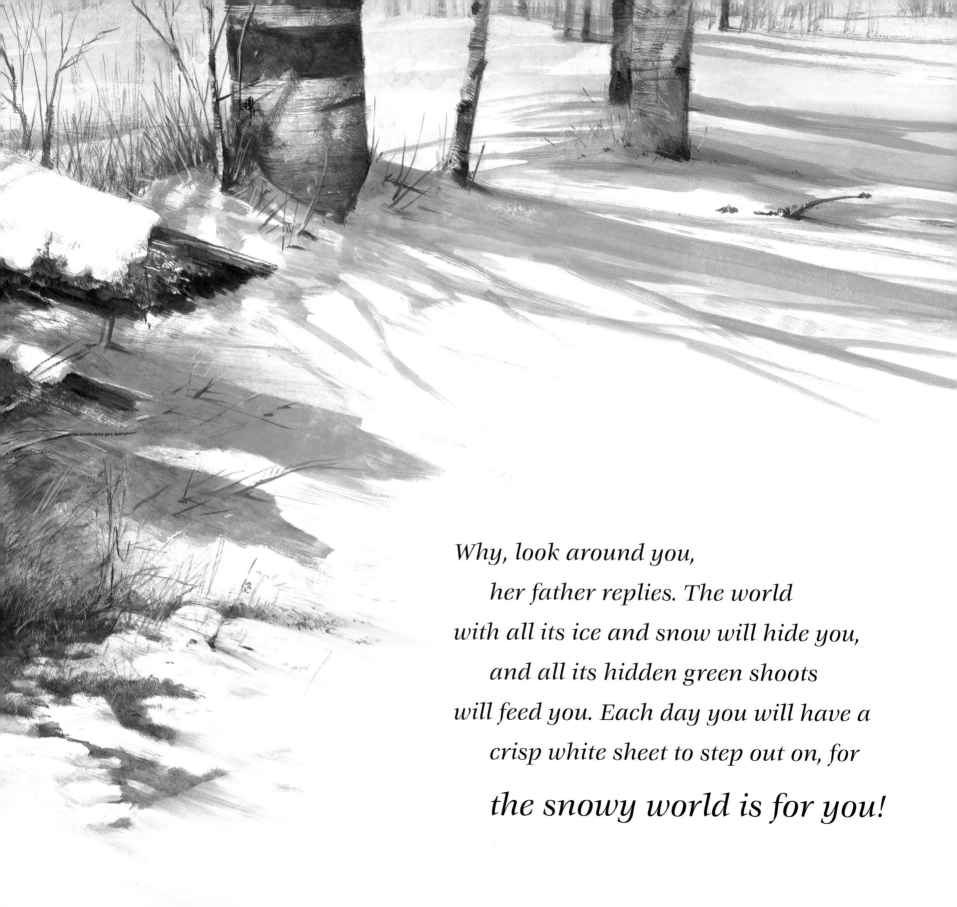

Why, look around you,
  her father replies. The world
with all its ice and snow will hide you,
  and all its hidden green shoots
will feed you. Each day you will have a
  crisp white sheet to step out on, for

the snowy world is for you!

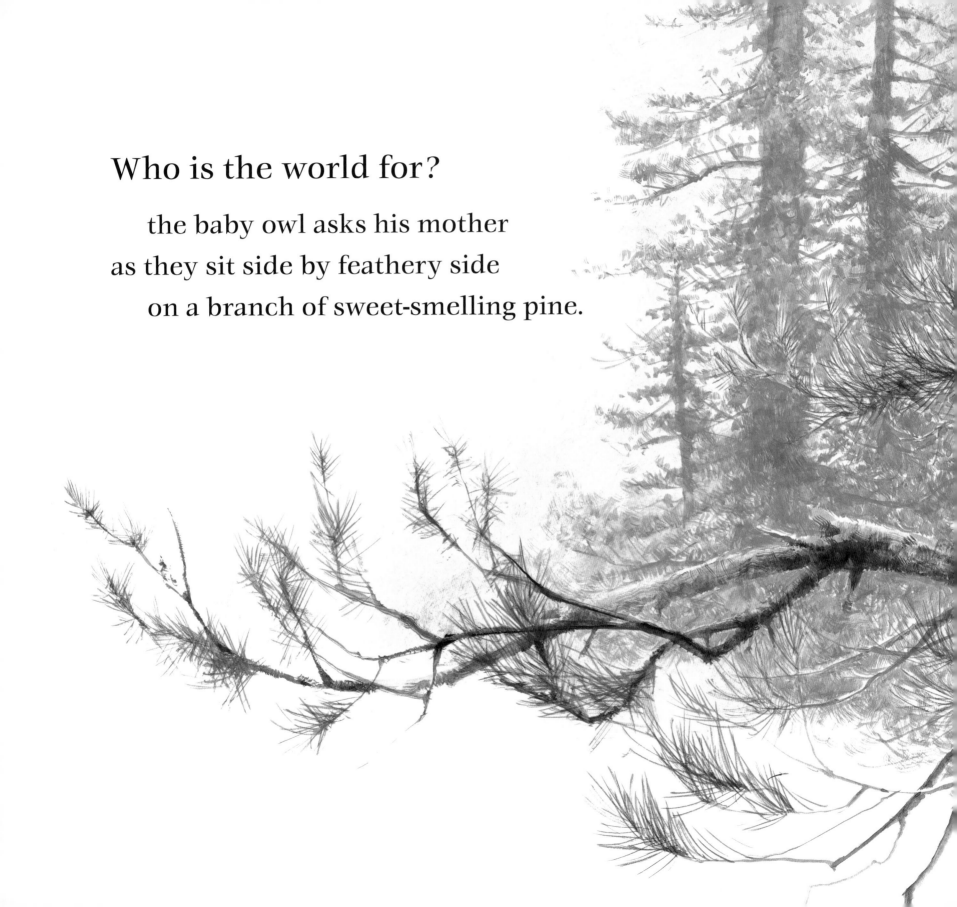

Who is the world for?

the baby owl asks his mother
as they sit side by feathery side
on a branch of sweet-smelling pine.

Why, look around you, his mother replies.

 The world with all its high green trees for you to hoot from
and with all its fence posts for you to perch on, all its moonbeams
 for you to swoop down on toward the tiniest rustling leaf~
 my dear, the world is a wood, and

the world is for you!

Who is the world for?

> the small boy asks his father
as they kneel side by side
> in a rumpled nest of blankets.

> *Why, the father replies,*
> > *the world is a very big place.*

And somewhere under its stars~

way, way out there~on a cold mountainside,

bear cubs curl up beside their mothers in dark warm caves;

lion cubs stretch out beside their fathers on a hot and dusty plain;

Arctic hares doze with slipper-soft babes in secret burrows of snow;

and closer, much closer to home~

listen!~
an owl hoots to her baby from the
middle of the dark green wood.

The world is for
all of these.

The boy leans into his father,
as together they look out
into the big starry night.

And is the world for people, too~
like me and you? he asks.

Oh yes, answers his father,
wherever they may live,
the world is for people, too.
The world is for everyone!

*But **my** world is here~with you.*
*And **our** world has parks for you*
to play in and rivers for you to cross.
It has hills for you to climb up high
and canyons and seashores to explore.

Already we have seen so much
yet we've much, much more
to see and do.

Who is the world for?

The world is
for you!